www.mascotbooks.com

For more information, please contact:
Mascot Books
560 Herndon Parkway #120
Herndon, VA 20170
info@mascotbooks.com

CPSIA Code: PRT0913A
ISBN-10: 1620862883
ISBN-13: 9781620862889

Printed in the United States

THAT'S NOT OUR MASCOT?

Smokey is Our Mascot

by Jason Wells and Jeff Wells

illustrated by Patrick Carlson

Who's that tailgating on the Tennessee River?

That's not our mascot...
it's Big Red, the Arkansas Razorback.

Who's that playing in the
Pride of the Southland Band?

That's not our mascot...
it's Aubie, the Auburn Tiger.

Who's that shooting hoops
in Thompson-Boling Arena?

That's not our mascot...
it's Scratch, the Kentucky Wildcat.

That's not our mascot...
it's Rebel, the Ole Miss Black Bear.

Who's that working out at T RECS?

That's not our mascot...
it's Bully, the Mississippi State Bulldog.

Who's that drawing on The Rock?

That's not our mascot...
it's Truman, the Missouri Tiger.

**Who's that studying
at Hodges Library?**

That's not our mascot...
it's Mike, the LSU Tiger.

Who's that playing on the Pedestrian Mall?

That's not our mascot...
it's Reveille from Texas A&M.

Who's that strolling
by Ayres Hall?

That's not our mascot...
it's Mr. C, the Vanderbilt® Commodore.